Going Camping

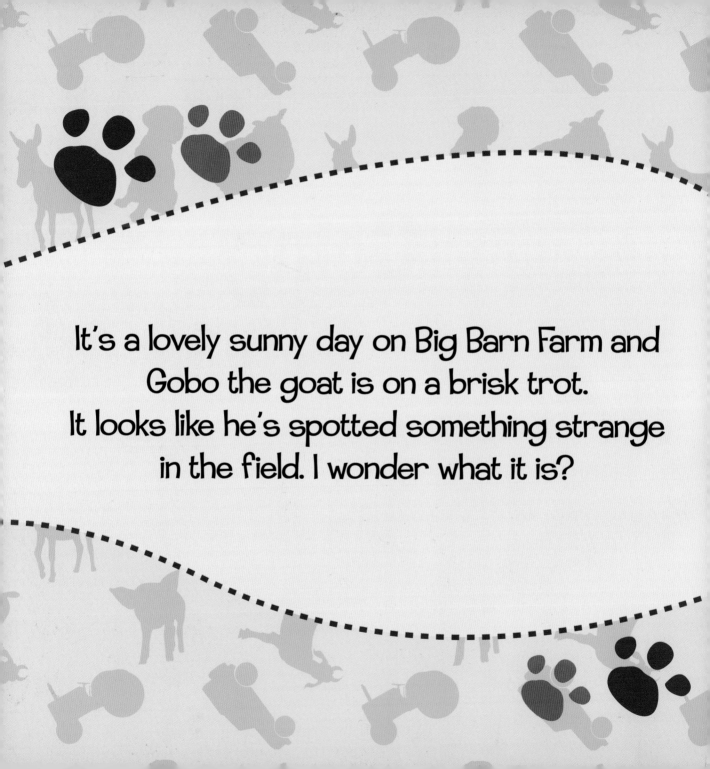

It's a lovely sunny day on Big Barn Farm and
Gobo the goat is on a brisk trot.
It looks like he's spotted something strange
in the field. I wonder what it is?

Gobo runs back to the farmyard to tell his friends Dash the donkey, Digger the puppy and Petal the piglet about the monster. "It's big, pointy and has legs, like a spider!"

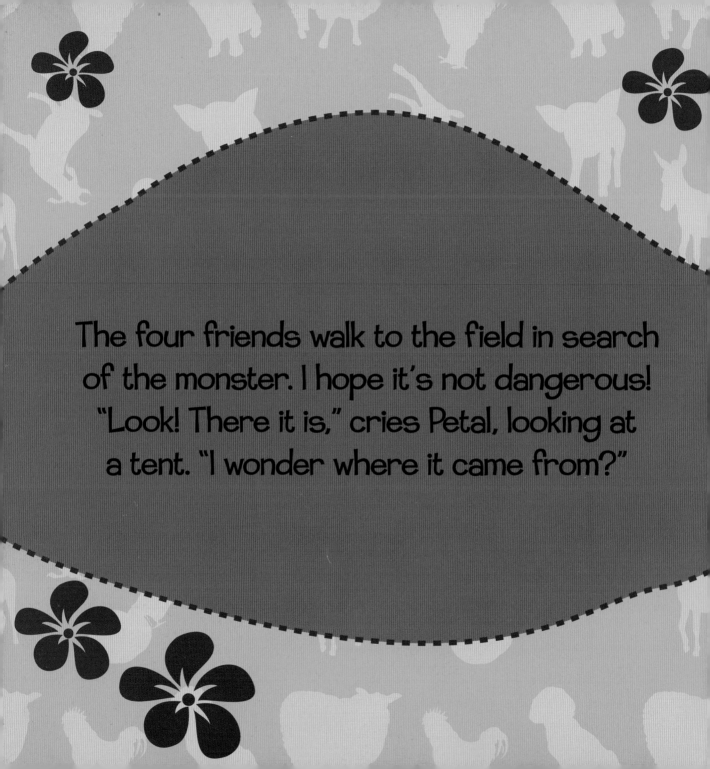

The four friends walk to the field in search of the monster. I hope it's not dangerous! "Look! There it is," cries Petal, looking at a tent. "I wonder where it came from?"

Suddenly, the tent opens and a man climbs out of it. The Farmyard Bunch are watching. "Oh dear! The monster has spat out a man. It must have tried to eat him!" cries Petal.

Just then, the man walks out of the field, leaving the Farmyard Bunch with his tent. "Hmmm," says Petal, looking at the tent. "It doesn't really look like a monster."

"Moo la la! What eez going on?" asks Madame the cow, arriving on the scene. "We've found a monster," replies Dash. "Zat eez not a monster. It eez a 'tent' - a house for humans!"

The Farmyard Bunch don't know what a tent is. "Why does it have a mouth?" asks Digger. "Zat eez not a mouth - it eez a door," explains Madame. "Do not touch it. It's not yours," adds Madame, leaving the friends by themselves.

Petal, Gobo and Digger ignore Madame's advice and climb inside the tent. "What's this metal thing?" says Gobo. "I'm going to pull it . . . " Oh dear! Gobo has zipped everyone inside the tent. How will they get out?

Gobo wonders how they can get out. "Maybe if I pull this shiny metal thing again," says Gobo, pulling the zip again and opening up the tent. Phew! Now they can get out.

The tent has lots of things for everyone to play with. Gobo tries to eat the sleeping bag, Digger makes the tent fall down and Petal uses the mobile phone! Oh no! They've made a right old mess, haven't they?

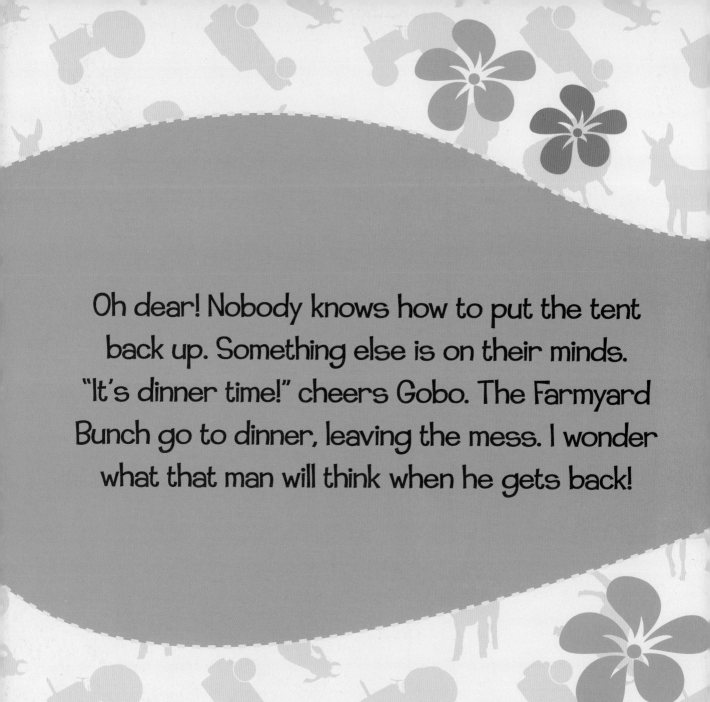

Oh dear! Nobody knows how to put the tent back up. Something else is on their minds. "It's dinner time!" cheers Gobo. The Farmyard Bunch go to dinner, leaving the mess. I wonder what that man will think when he gets back!